ELI
the
BAD SPELLER

by ROBERT KRAUS

Silver Press

Library of Congress Cataloging-in-Publication Data

Kraus, Robert, 1925–
    Ella the bad speller / story and illustrations by
Robert Kraus.
        p.   cm.—(Miss Gator's schoolhouse; bk. 2)
    Summary: Ella the elephant, the worst speller in
Miss Gator's schoolhouse, works very hard with the
help of the other animals to improve her spelling.
    [1. English language—Spelling—Fiction.
2. Elephants—Fiction.   3. Animals—Fiction.
4. Schools—Fiction.]   I. Title.   II. Series: Kraus,
Robert, 1925-   Miss Gator's schoolhouse; bk. 2.
PZ7.K868E1   1989
[E]—dc19   89-6096
ISBN 0-671-68606-2 (lib. bdg.)   CIP
ISBN 0-671-68610-0 (pbk.)   AC

Produced by Parachute Press, Inc.
Published by Silver Press, a division of
Silver Burdett Press, Inc.
Simon & Schuster, Inc.,
Prentice Hall Bldg., Englewood Cliffs, NJ 07632.
Printed in the United States of America.
10 9 8 7 6 5 4 3 2

Chapter 1
ALL ABOUT ELLA

Ella was a bad speller.

She couldn't spell anything right.

She spelled everything wrong.

She spelled Dog

C–A–T.

She spelled Cat

D–O–G.

"Oh, what am I going to do
with you, Ella?"
sighed Miss Gator.
"How will I ever teach you
to spell?"

"The Spelling Bee is coming up
next week," said Ella's
best friend, Punky Skunky.
"I really want to win it!"
said Ella.
"But, Ella, you can't spell,"
said Punky.

"I'm going to study hard
and do my best," said Ella.
"Where there's a will,
there's a way," said Punky,
giving Ella a hug.

So every day Ella studied hard
while her friends played.

And every night Ella studied
hard while her friends slept.

But did it help?

No.

Ella was still a bad speller.

"Maybe Ella should watch more
TV," said Ella's father.
"What's wrong with that kid
anyway?
She always has her trunk
in a book."

"Ella wants to win the Spelling
Bee," said Ella's mother,
"but she can't even spell
her own name."

So Ella's mother and father
went to talk to Miss Gator
about Ella's problem.

"Glad you could come,"
said Miss Gator.
"Talking to parents can be
so helpful."

"I don't know where Ella
got her problem,"
said Ella's father.
"She didn't get it from
me, M–E–E.
I was always a good
speller, S–P–E–L–E–R."

"She didn't get it from me,"
said Ella's mother.
"Spelling was always my best
subject, S–U–B–G–E–C–T."

15

"Don't worry," said Miss Gator.
"The class and I will work
with Ella.
We'll teach her how to spell,
or my name isn't Miss Gator."

Chapter 2
HELPING ELLA

Everybody in Miss Gator's
class tried to help Ella
become a good speller.
It wasn't easy.

Punky Skunky was the coolest

kid in the class.

She taught Ella how to spell

cool words like

Snow,

Ice,

and

Sleet.

Buggy Bear, who never took
baths, taught Ella how to spell
buggy words like
Itchy
and
Scratchy.

Blake the Snake taught Ella

how to spell snaky words like

Sneak,

Snoop,

and

Snitch.

Tardy Toad taught Ella how

to spell tardy words like

Late,

Later,

and

Latest.

Miss Gator gave Ella a set of
alphabet cards.
She showed Ella how to spell
out words with them.

Ella loved the cards.

She carried them with her

all the time.

Ella even slept with the cards

under her pillow.

And she dreamed about letters

at night.

Everybody wanted to win
the Spelling Bee.
They all studied very hard
in class.

24

And they all studied very
hard at home.

Nobody studied harder

than Ella.

But no matter how hard she
tried, Ella still couldn't spell
the simplest words.

The day before the Spelling

Bee, Miss Gator said,

"You've all studied very hard,

and I'm very proud of you.

But now I want you all

to go home and get

a good night's sleep.

May the best speller win."

Chapter 3
THE BIG SPELLING BEE

At last it was the day

of the big Spelling Bee.

Miss Gator got up

at the crack of her back.

She hopped into her speedboat
and zoomed across the swamp
to her little one-room
schoolhouse.

Ella's parents saw her

off to school.

"Spell right, R–I–T–E,"

said Ella's dad.

"I'll do my best," said Ella.

Buggy Bear washed his face.

He wanted to be clean

for the contest.

Punky Skunky combed her hair.

She wanted to be cute

for the contest.

Blake the Snake
did the Twist.
He wanted to
loosen up
for the contest.

But Tardy Toad didn't do
anything.
He was fast asleep.
He had forgotten to set
his alarm clock.

At eight o'clock sharp,
Miss Gator rang the bell.
"Good morning, class,"
said Miss Gator.
"Good morning, Miss Gator,"
said the class.

Everybody was present—
except Tardy Toad.

"We'll just have to start
without him," said Miss Gator.
"The first word is
Constantinople!"

The class groaned.

"Con-standy-what???" said
Buggy Bear.

"Con-standy-apple!" hissed
Blake the Snake.

"No talking, please,"
said Miss Gator.

"Punky Skunky, you're first."

"K–O–N–S–T–A–N–T–I–N–O–O–D–L–E,"
spelled Punky.

"Sorry," said Miss Gator.

"Better luck next time."

"You're next, Blake."

"C-O-N-S-T-A-N-T-I-N-O-O-D-L-E,"
spelled Blake.

"Sorry, Blake," said Miss Gator.

"Nice try."

"Thanks, Miss Gator,"

said Blake.

Miss Gator always put things

in such a nice way

no one ever felt bad.

"Next!" Miss Gator called.

"K-A-A-K-A-N-S-T-A-N-A-P-P-L-E,"
spelled Buggy, scratching
his head.

Poor Ella.

She was so nervous.

She kept shuffling her
alphabet cards while
she waited for her turn.

Tardy Toad came rushing in.

"What's the word?

What's the word?" he asked.

"You're late," said Miss Gator.

"As usual.

And the word is

Constantinople."

"I can't spell it," said Tardy.

"And I'm too late to try."

"Sorry," said Miss Gator.

"Next!"

"That leaves you, Ella,"
said Miss Gator.

"Oh, dear, D–E–E–R," said Ella.

Now she was more nervous
than ever.

"I know I can't.

I know I can't.

I know I can't," Ella cried.

Ella threw up her hands
in despair.

All of her alphabet cards
flew into the air...

CONSTANT

Then one by one,

they fell to the floor.

And this is how they landed.

C-O-N-S-T-A-N-T-I-N-O-P-L-E!

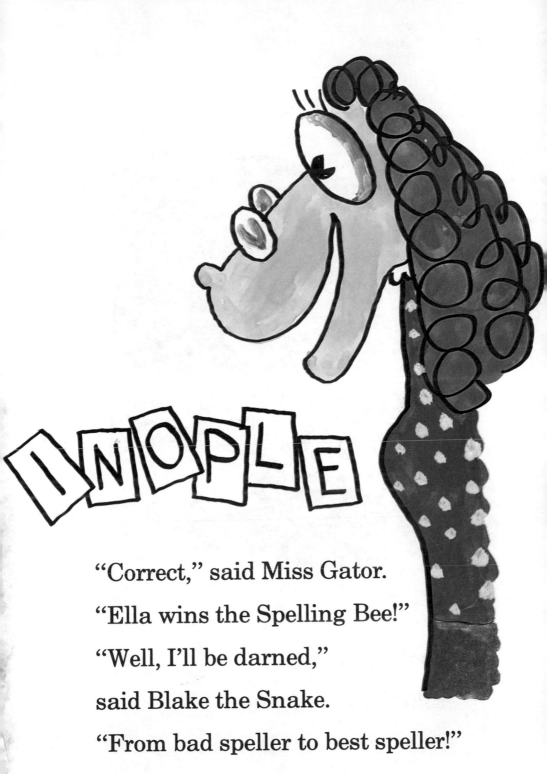

"Correct," said Miss Gator.

"Ella wins the Spelling Bee!"

"Well, I'll be darned,"

said Blake the Snake.

"From bad speller to best speller!"

So that's how

Ella the Bad Speller

won Miss Gator's Spelling Bee.